RIVER FISH

JANE LANDEY

SPECIAL EDITION
Copyrights©2015
All rights reserved.
ISBN-13: 978-1514392911
Printed in U.S.A.

Introduction

This is a special edition of River Fish. A fish that l o v e d the river it lived and the sea nearby. One day, it sadly got hooked by a fisherman.

River Fish

There lived a fish in a river.

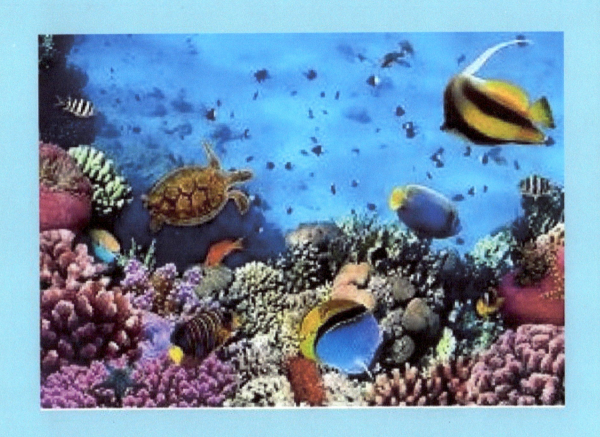

There was a big sea nearby.

The river ran into the sea.

River Fish loved it in the blue sea.

It swam into the sea.

It loved to see the ships sailed by.

It ate the jelly fishes.

They ran away when it came near them!

It knew when a ship was coming.

Oh, look at this big ship!

It swam closer to see how big it was.

On the ship was a big house.

Oh, how I love to see the inside!

It looked at the ship until it sailed off.

River fish loved some other things too!

It hid in between rocks.

No one could see it.

It played by the sea too!

Some days, ships did not sail by.

Some days, it could see only boats.

The boats stayed on the sea for days.

The men did not see him.

It was happy when they went away!

It stopped raining.

Ships and boats did not sail by.

River fish became sad.

It wished to see the big ships.

30

It sat all days long.

No ship was sailing by!

One morning, it swam to the sea.

It was expecting a ship.

Suddenly, a boat was speeding towards it.

There was a man with a hook.

What could that be? It thought.

It was too late for River Fish.

Look at this beautiful raft!

It stared at it until it moved far away.

The fisherman swung his hook.

River Fish tried to escape.

It caught river fish on the mouth.

Oh, do not take me away!

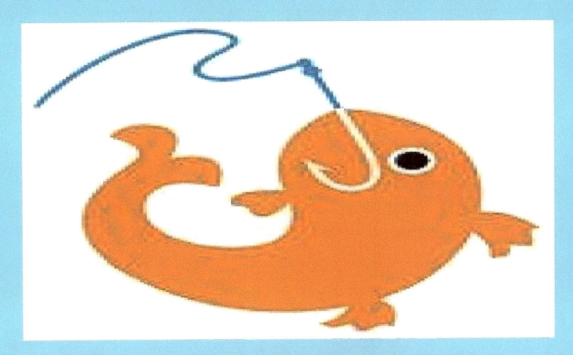

I always love it here!

The fisherman did not listen to River Fish.

He carried it to his house.

River Fish tried to jump.

Let me go! Let me go!!

He begged the fisherman.

My name is River Fish.

I want to go back to the river.

He took a knife and raised River Fish up.

He opened the gills.

The fisherman gasped.

There were coins and paper money coming out of his mouth!

He took the coins and paper money and cooked River Fish!

The fisherman became a rich man!

Thus the end of River Fish!

Other Brim Children Storybooks
Have you read all of them?

The princess and the rain

The House in the Moon

Mr. Oak and the hunters

Spring party

Howling wind

Mr. Fox in the Cave

Blue star and its little ones

Rabbit and the burning grass

River Fish
Jane Landey

CPSIA information can be obtained
at www.ICGtesting.com
Printed in the USA
LVHW072007190122
708922LV00002B/45